MAY 1993

BRYAN, Jenny. *Breathing: The Respiratory System.* ISBN 0-87518-563-0. LC 92-36353.

———. *Digestion: The Digestive System.* ISBN 0-87518-564-0. LC 92-35052.

———. *Movement: The Muscular and Skeletal System.* ISBN 0-87518-565-7. LC 92-35092.

———. *The Pulse of Life: The Circulatory System.* ISBN 0-87518-566-5. LC 92-36410.

ea. vol: 48p. diags. photos. reprods. further reading. glossary. index. (Body Talk Series). CIP. Dillon: Macmillan. 1993. PLB $13.95.

Gr 4-6—What at first glance seems to be yet another British import series on human anatomy, is in fact something quite different. Instead of merely presenting information on the structure and function of the body's various systems, Bryan branches out to include a wide range of related and peripheral topics, along with associated health problems currently being investigated. Of necessity, coverage is limited to a couple of paragraphs. For example, *Movement* begins with a description of the two types of muscles and how they function. Bones and muscles working together is exemplified by the inner ear. What follows is a discus-

Continued

This is an uncorrected proof of a review scheduled for School Library Journal, Oct., 1993

BODY TALK

BREATHING

THE RESPIRATORY SYSTEM

JENNY BRYAN

Dillon Press
New York

B O D Y   T A L K

BREATHING

DIGESTION

MIND AND MATTER

MOVEMENT

THE PULSE OF LIFE

REPRODUCTION

SMELL, TASTE AND TOUCH

SOUND AND VISION

Editor: Catherine Baxter
Series Design: Loraine Hayes
Consultant: Dr. Tony Smith, Associate Editor of the *British Medical Journal*
Cover and title page: Diver with oxygen tank

First Dillon Press edition 1993

Dillon Press
Macmillan Publishing Company
866 Third Avenue
New York, NY 10022

Macmillan Publishing Company is part of the Maxwell Communication Group of Companies.

First published in 1992 by Wayland (Publishers) Limited
61 Western Road, Hove, East Sussex, England BN3 1JD

Library of Congress Cataloging in Publication Data

Bryan, Jenny.
   Breathing : the respiratory system / Jenny Bryan.
      p.   cm. — (Body talk)
   Includes index.
   Summary: Describes how the respiratory system works and discusses such related topics as smoking, air polution, asthma, cystic fibrosis, and artificial ventilation.
   ISBN 0-87518-563-0
   1. Respiration—Juvenile literature. [1. Respiratory system. 2. Respiration.]   I. Title.   II. Series.
QP121.B87   1993
612.2—dc20   92-36353

Printed by G. Canale C.S.p.A., Turin, Italy

10 9 8 7 6 5 4 3 2 1

CONTENTS

INTRODUCTION

WANTED: two spongy bags for gas processing. Must be highly flexible and able to work under great pressure. Very long-term contract. Should expect to be mistreated.

Not a very attractive job description, is it? But those are the conditions under which our lungs must work. They must inflate and deflate about 20,000 times a day, 365 days a year, so that air can enter our bodies and provide a constant supply of life-giving oxygen to our cells.

The same principles of breathing can be seen in all birds, mammals, fish, and insects, although the mechanisms may vary. Oxygen is taken out of the air, taken into the bloodstream, carried to all the cells in the body, and used to produce energy. Waste gas—carbon dioxide—is then carried back to the lungs and expelled into the atmosphere.

Humans breathe in through their noses and, sometimes, their mouths. The nose is better designed for the job, since it warms and filters the air before it passes down into the throat (pharynx) and on through the voice box (larynx).

Below the throat, two long tubes lie alongside each other. One—the trachea—carries air to the lungs. The other—the esophagus—carries food to the stomach. So that there is no mistake, the opening to the voice box has a cover called the epiglottis. This flips open to allow air down but slams shut to keep food out.

At its lower end, the trachea splits into two. One tube—the left bronchus—goes to the left lung, and the right bronchus takes air to the right lung. Each bronchus divides into smaller and smaller passages, called bronchioles. At the end of the smallest tubes are tiny air sacs, called alveoli, where the real business of gas processing goes on.

It is the alveoli that pay the price for our thoughtlessness. They must deal with the gases from car exhausts and factory chimneys. They are also assaulted every day by the poisonous chemicals in cigarette smoke.

No wonder those bouncy sponges that start out as efficient gas processors often end up worn out and unable to give the body the oxygen it needs.

This is what the insides of your lungs look like. The large opening at the left of the picture is a bronchiole. The smaller, spongy sections on the right are the alveoli, where gas exchange takes place. You can see how fragile the tissue is and how easily it might be damaged.

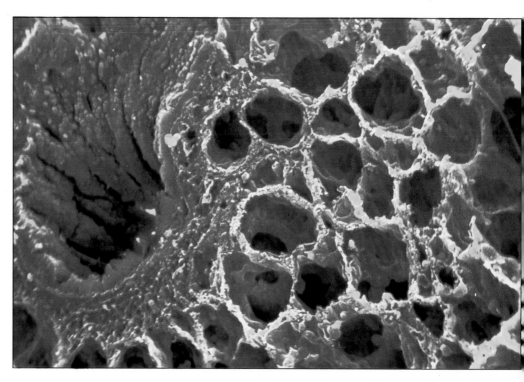

The respiratory system

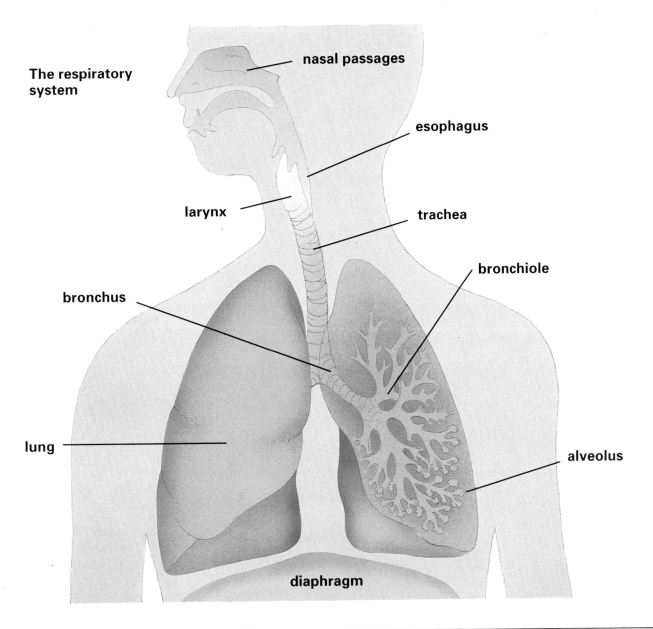

nasal passages

esophagus

larynx

trachea

bronchiole

bronchus

lung

alveolus

diaphragm

RIGHT These are lungs from sheep. The healthy-looking lungs on the left came from an Australian sheep. The diseased lungs on the right came from a Kuwaiti sheep. It died as a result of inhaling large amounts of crude oil from the wells left burning by retreating Iraqi soldiers at the end of the 1991 Gulf War.

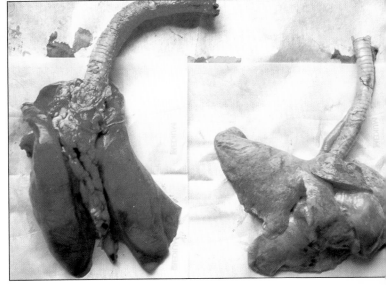

THE FIRST BREATH

Before birth a fetus relies on its mother's blood to take oxygen to its cells and carry carbon dioxide away. Its lungs are filled with fluid and don't have to breathe, although they do take a few practice breaths as birth approaches.

At birth, a baby's lungs must fill with air for the first time. The baby can't do this on his or her own. Breathing is controlled by muscles that let the chest expand and the lungs inflate.

First, the baby's brain realizes that oxygen is no longer coming from the mother and it must act quickly to start the baby breathing. The brain sends messages down nerves to the intercostal muscles between the ribs and the diaphragm—a sheet of muscle that lies below the lungs and separates the chest from the stomach. Occasionally something goes wrong at this stage, so doctors keep respiratory equipment close at hand.

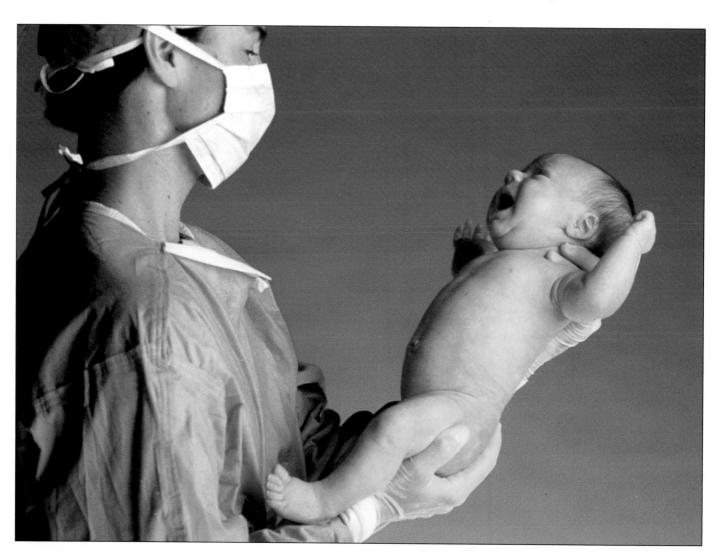

This baby's first cries have helped open up his lungs and start him breathing.

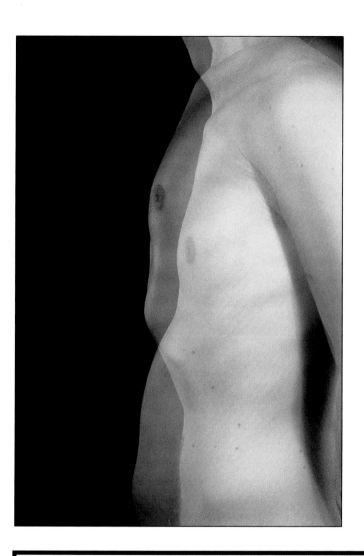

But, all being well, these messages tell the intercostal muscles to pull the rib cage outward and the diaphragm to relax downward so the space in the chest gets bigger. This makes the pressure in the chest go down to less than atmospheric pressure, so air rushes in to fill the lungs.

To breathe out, the muscles go into reverse. The space in the chest gets smaller and the pressure rises, pushing air out of the lungs. The whole process then begins all over again.

If the insides of the lungs were dry, the effort needed to inflate them would be too much for the baby. Cells in the lungs continually make a detergentlike substance, called surfactant. This lubricates the lungs and makes it easier for the inner surfaces to slide over one another and open up to let air in.

LEFT Look how far the chest expands when you breathe in and the abdomen extends when you breathe out. All the movements depend on the muscles between the ribs and the diaphragm—which is below the rib cage.

WHEN THE LUNGS ARE TOO SMALL

One in 100 babies is born with a condition called respiratory distress syndrome. This means that their lungs have not fully developed and they cannot produce enough surfactant. The problem is most common in premature babies, especially those born ten or more weeks too early. Without enough surfactant, the premature baby is simply not strong enough to breathe. So it has to be attached to a machine, called a ventilator, which breathes for it (right).

Recently, doctors have discovered how to make surfactant. So premature babies can be given it to help them breathe. Twenty years ago, about half the babies born with respiratory distress syndrome died. But thanks to modern treatment, including surfactant therapy, 90 percent now survive.

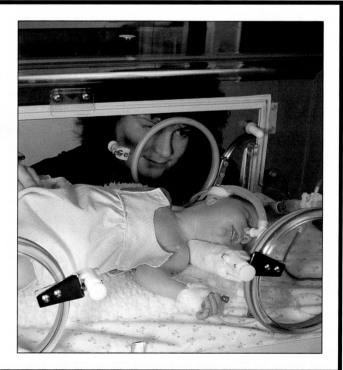

HOW AIR GETS INTO THE BLOOD

An average human lung contains about 300 million alveoli. If all the alveoli in both lungs were spread out, they would cover an area about the size of a tennis court!

Crisscrossing the walls of all the tiny alveoli are even tinier hairlike blood vessels called capillaries. It is through these that oxygen is absorbed into the bloodstream and carbon dioxide passed back into the lungs. The walls of the alveoli are paper thin. This means that the molecules of oxygen and carbon dioxide have to travel only a tiny distance to get in and out of the blood.

Oxygen and carbon dioxide do not simply float around in the blood. They are carried around by red blood cells on a chemical called hemoglobin. This is also the pigment that makes blood red.

Blood arrives in the capillaries of the alveoli from the right side of the heart. This means it has

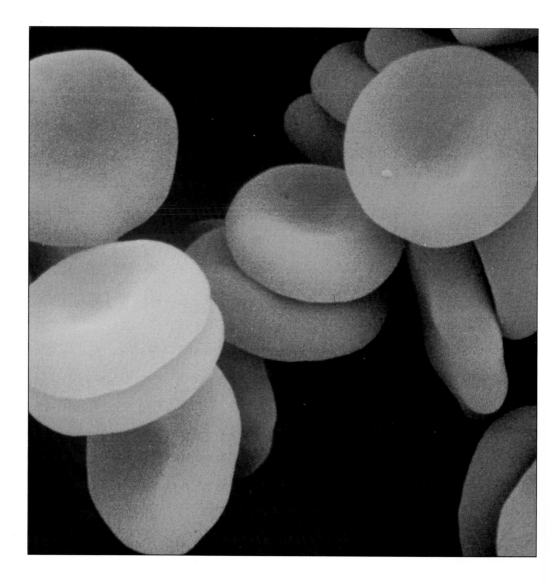

This photograph of red blood cells was taken under a microscope. A false color was then added to make the cells show up. Mature red blood cells carry oxygen around the body. Their shape enables maximum amounts of oxygen and carbon dioxide to be exchanged.

All day, every day, gas exchange goes on across the walls of the capillaries of the alveoli deep inside the lungs. As one lot of newly oxygenated blood sets off back to the heart, ready to go around the body, the next batch arrives ready to unload its carbon dioxide and take on fresh supplies of oxygen.

already been all around the body and its oxygen has been used up and converted into carbon dioxide ready to be breathed out.

The capillaries are so narrow that the red cells have to squeeze through. This means that they are pressed against the capillary walls and that oxygen and carbon dioxide swap places. Molecules of carbon dioxide come out of the red blood cells across the capillary walls and into the alveoli in exchange for oxygen molecules, which go in the opposite direction.

Oxygen is then carried back to the left side of the heart ready to be pumped around the body and carbon dioxide is breathed out.

WHAT'S IN AIR?

The air you breathe in is 78 percent nitrogen, 21 percent oxygen, and 0.04 percent carbon dioxide. The air you breathe out contains slightly more nitrogen, 16.4 percent oxygen, and 4 percent carbon dioxide.

There are also small amounts of pollutants in the air that you breathe. These include nitrogen dioxide and sulphur dioxide, which can be harmful, especially to people with lung problems. The exact amounts of these pollutants that are in the air depend on where you live and what the weather is like at the time.

WHY WE NEED OXYGEN

Your cells, your dog's cells, and your goldfish's cells, need oxygen. Without oxygen in the air, life as we know it would come to an end.

Blood that has picked up oxygen in the lungs is pumped to all parts of the body through smaller and smaller blood vessels until it reaches more tiny capillaries. There, oxygen spreads out into nearby cells and carbon dioxide diffuses back into the capillaries.

All cells need oxygen to produce chemical energy. They need this energy for the millions of jobs they do every single day.

You don't need to be moving around for your cells to need energy. Everything you do— breathing, eating, digesting, and blinking—needs energy. In fact, you even need energy to think. It is not the sort of amounts that you use up in a game of hockey or tennis but it is energy just the same.

Without oxygen, cells soon die. A few minutes without any oxygen can cause irreparable damage to the brain and other organs. Even a small reduction in oxygen can leave you panting for breath, weak, and dizzy.

GIVING OXYGEN

In some lung diseases, the alveoli become less efficient at taking oxygen from the air. But if they are given extra oxygen, they can make up the shortfall. Some people can get by with a few puffs from an oxygen cylinder every few hours. But others rely on oxygen concentrators to provide them with oxygen for several hours a day.

These machines take oxygen from the air and feed it through a long tube into the nose. They are very efficient and, with their long tubing, allow people to move around freely while getting all the oxygen they need.

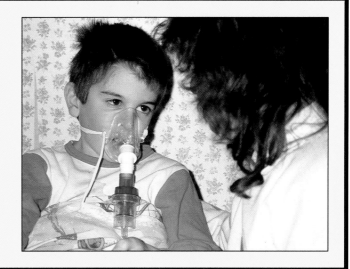

RIGHT Even when we are resting, we still need oxygen.

LEFT When you are exercising, you breathe faster in order to get the oxygen needed to produce lots of energy.

BREATHING PROPERLY

Children breathe faster than adults. A newborn baby breathes about thirty times a minute, but an adult breathes at about half that rate. When you are sitting quietly, you are probably taking in about 30 cubic inches of air in each breath—more than enough to fill a milk carton. But if you ran down the street to catch a bus, you could be breathing in as much as 6,100 cubic inches per minute.

Top athletes can do even better. Running flat out, some take between forty and sixty breaths a minute and breathe in over 12,200 cubic inches of air during that time. They don't have bigger lungs than the rest of us but are better at taking in air and getting oxygen. From 6,100 to 9,150 cubic inches of air, they could get around 305 cubic inches of oxygen for energy production.

When you are breathing quietly, about two-thirds of the air you breathe in actually gets down into your lungs. The rest stays in your mouth, trachea, and bronchi.

Top athletes, such as Jamaican sprinter Merlene Ottey, have to learn to breathe properly.

Your lungs always have some air in them, even between breaths. Otherwise, they would collapse. At any one time there are about 92 cubic inches of air in the lungs—easily enough to fill three milk cartons. The maximum amount that you can breathe in will depend on how much you can breathe out. When learning to breathe more efficiently, athletes practice breathing out, rather than breathing in. You could bear this in mind when training for sports at school.

Singers and public speakers also have to learn to breathe more efficiently. They need to be able to breathe in large amounts of air so that they don't have to take any quick breaths when they are in midsentence. They learn to breathe from their diaphragms. They squeeze out as much air as possible and then feel their lungs fill from the bottom up.

People who can't get enough air into their lungs soon become breathless. Their lungs inflate and deflate more and more quickly as they try to get more air. But this leaves them with less and less time to breathe deeply. They get no more air, but their breathing becomes much more of an effort. This, in turn, means that they use more energy in breathing and the shortage of oxygen gets worse. People with long-term breathing problems feel very tired and cannot move around normally because they do not have enough energy.

ABOVE Opera singer Luciano Pavarotti is able to sustain very long notes because he has learned to fill his lungs totally with air between musical phrases. By breathing from his diaphragm, he makes his lungs work more efficiently.

CHECKING YOUR BREATHING
Using the second hand of your watch or a stopwatch, count the number of times you breathe in a minute when you are sitting still doing nothing. Then do some steady exercise that you know you can keep up for about fifteen minutes. Stop every five minutes and measure your breathing rate. Then measure your breathing rate when you stop exercising and every three minutes for the next fifteen minutes.

See how high your breathing rate goes when it reaches a maximum and how quickly it returns to normal after you stop your exercise. The sooner you are breathing normally, the more fit you are.

THE BRAIN AND BREATHING

Your brain can't just guess when to tell you to breathe in and out. It has to be told when you need oxygen. This job is done by receptors in the walls of some of your blood vessels. Just as the dipstick in the engine of a car will tell you when you are running low on oil, so these receptors tell the brain when levels of carbon dioxide are getting too high. A warning signal is sent to the breathing center in the brain. This then sends messages down the nerves to the lungs and the diaphragm telling them

that it's time to breathe in some more air so that the oxygen supply to the rest of the body is increased.

As the lungs expand, a second set of receptors, in the bronchioles and alveoli, go into action. These are called stretch receptors. It is their job to send messages to the brain when the lungs are full of air. The brain realizes that enough air has been breathed in and sends messages back to the lungs and diaphragm telling them to relax so that you can breathe out.

LEFT Playing a wind or brass instrument requires very efficient breathing and expert timing.

RIGHT This little boy makes it look so easy! But swimming underwater requires careful control of your breathing.

Most of the time you won't even be aware that you are breathing in and out. Your lungs just work automatically. Your brain will tell them when to inflate and when to deflate, without your having to think about it.

Sometimes you may want to take over the breathing. If you are at the beach, for example, you may want to take lots of deep breaths of fresh air. Or if you are diving, you may want to hold your breath.

You can do all of these things and your brain will gladly oblige by telling your lungs to adapt their breathing pattern. But if you deliberately breathe too fast—hyperventilate—you will confuse the whole system.

As you breathe harder and harder, you will breathe out more and more carbon dioxide, so levels in your bloodstream will go down. Your receptors—not sensing much carbon dioxide—will not tell your brain that you need to breathe. You will stop breathing and the lack of carbon dioxide in your blood will make it more alkaline. This will make your muscles go into spasm.

This is what happens during hysteria. Hysteria makes people hyperventilate. They fall to the ground twitching and gasping as their brains try to make sense of the signals they are receiving. Hyperventilation can be counteracted by breathing into a paper (not plastic) bag.

CRIB DEATHS

Each year about 2,000 babies die as a result of "crib death." They seem healthy when they go to bed at night. But they are found dead in the morning. No one knows quite why this happens. But it has been shown that some babies stop breathing for long periods of time when they are asleep. There must be something wrong with the mechanism that should tell their brains when they need to breathe. In some cases, they do not start breathing again without help. Babies known to be at risk can be fitted with special alarms to awaken their parents. Parents are also advised to lay their babies on their sides.

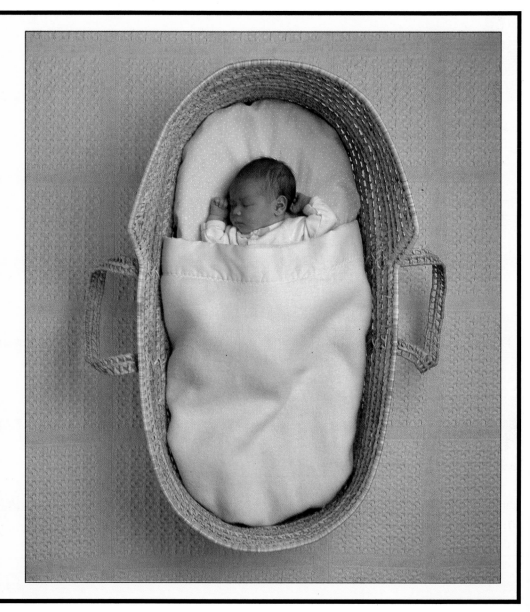

THE NOSE

We don't just use our noses to smell things. Before it reaches the lungs, the air we breathe has been through the quality control system in our noses, where it has been cleaned, warmed, and given the "all clear" signal.

The nose acts as a filter and heating system for the lungs. Hairs in the nostrils trap dirt in the air and prevent it from going down into the lungs. Cells in the lining of the nose produce sticky mucus, which captures any particles that have escaped the hairs. Then, as the air goes up the nose, warmth from the blood in the tiny blood vessels in the nose helps to raise the temperature of the air.

Inside the bones around the bridge of the nose are four sets of air-filled cavities called sinuses. These also produce mucus and help prepare the air for its journey down to the lungs.

When you have a cold, the inside of your nose becomes swollen and vast amounts of mucus are produced. This is the nose's way of defending itself from attack by the germs that cause colds. But it is very uncomfortable for us.

A growing number of people have "allergic" noses. Their noses respond in the same way to harmless things in the air, such as pollen, dust, and animal fur, as they do to germs. They become red and swollen and filled with lots of mucus.

If nothing is done, the mucus can fill and eventually block the sinuses. This can happen after a cold or because of an allergy. If mucus is trapped in the sinuses for a long time, it can become infected. Blocked sinuses can be very painful. Sufferers ache around their eyes and sometimes across much of their faces.

If you know people who seem to have colds all the time, they may well have allergic noses. If they are worse in summer, they are probably suffering from hay fever. And if they complain of being permanently stuffed up, it is possible that they have sinusitis.

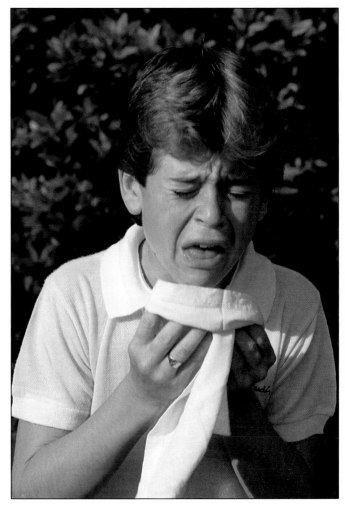

ABOVE Hay fever can make you pretty miserable. But there are pills and sprays that can help stop your nose from running.

LEFT Inhaling steam is an old remedy for a blocked nose. But it can be quite effective. The towel stops the steam from escaping.

UNBLOCKING NOSES

Sometimes blowing your nose is all you need to do to get rid of mucus. But if your nose is filled up, there are other simple remedies. Nose drops may stop the swelling in the nose or dry up some of the mucus. Steam treatment can also make your nose less blocked up.

COLDS AND FLU

Each time you sneeze, you spray the air around you with thousands of droplets of saliva and mucus. If you have a cold or flu, the droplets will contain the germs that cause those infections and you'll pass them on to other people.

A cold can be caused by any one of 200 different viruses. There are fewer flu viruses, but year by year they are able to change slightly, so they can be even more of a nuisance than cold viruses. Some of them can make you feel terrible!

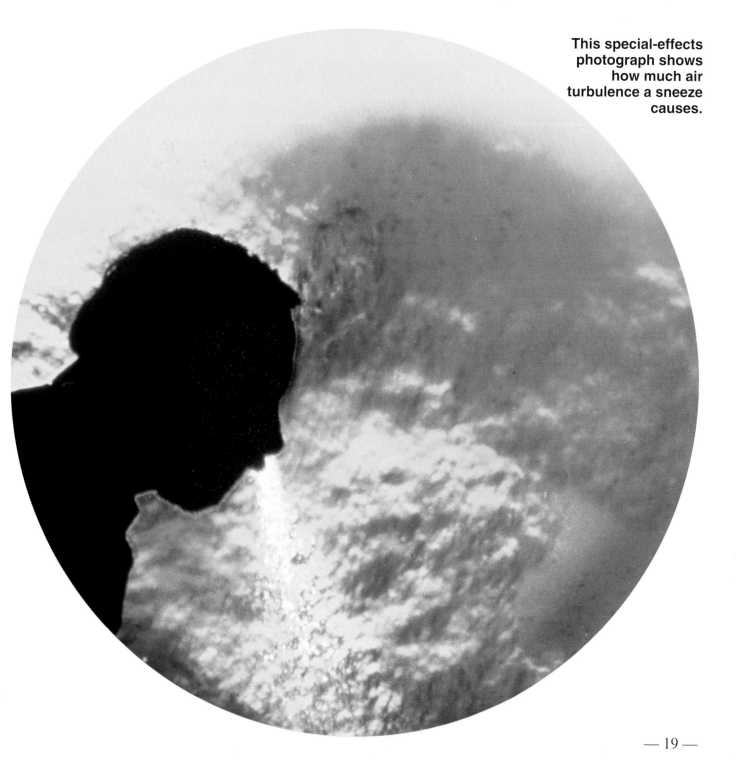

This special-effects photograph shows how much air turbulence a sneeze causes.

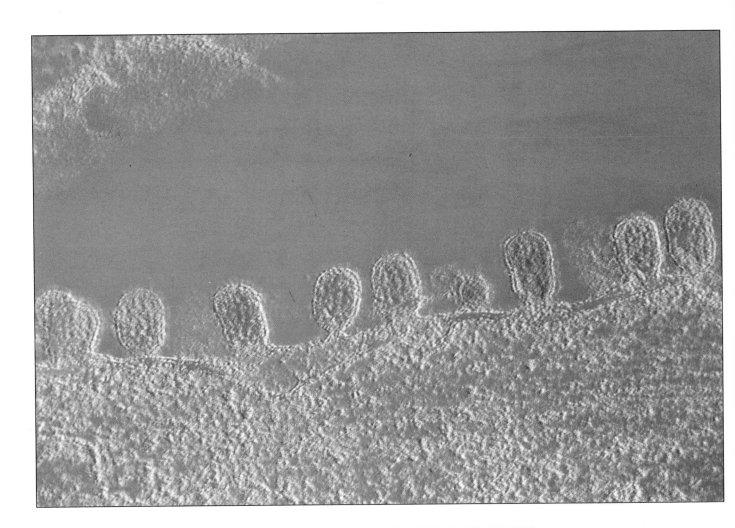

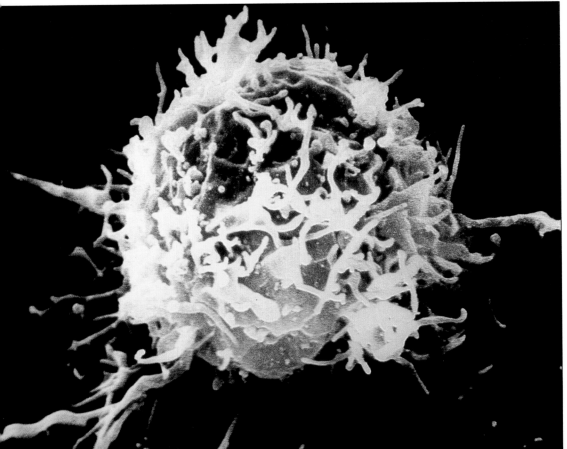

ABOVE This picture has had color added to show particles of flu virus sitting on the surface of a cell, preparing to invade nearby cells.

LEFT This T-lymphocyte is the type of white blood cell that stands between you and nasty infections. But its spiky appearance won't be enough to scare off bacteria and viruses. It will need help from other immune cells.

Viruses are so tiny that you can't see any of them —not even through a typical school microscope. In fact, a bacterium is fifty times larger. A virus does not have its own cell to live in. It just consists of a piece of genetic material—DNA or RNA— and an outer coating of protein.

Cold and flu viruses spend most of their time invading human cells. When you breathe in virus-containing droplets, the viruses quickly get into the cells of your nose. They head for the nucleus in the center of your cells, where your own DNA is. Here, they quickly multiply and move on to attack the next cells.

Your body responds by activating your natural defenses—your immune system. First on the scene are the white blood cells. They attack the viruses and produce proteins called antibodies. These antibodies not only attack viruses, but also call in other cells to attack them, too. With all this activity, the lining of your nose becomes swollen and you need lots of tissues as you produce large quantities of mucus.

Over the next few days a fierce battle is fought inside your nose and probably your throat. Eventually, the cold or flu virus loses and your own cells win.

If you have flu, the battle will probably spread farther down, into your trachea and bronchi, and take longer to win. Your body temperature will rise and your head, your arms, and your legs may ache. Scientists aren't sure whether the rise in temperature is part of the body's defense plan aimed at making life too hot for the viruses or the result of the viral attack.

IN SEARCH OF A CURE

There is no cure for either a cold or flu. Painkillers will help relieve the aches and pains and bring your temperature down. Decongestants will help unblock your nose. But scientists have not yet found any drugs that are effective against cold and flu viruses.

Antibiotic drugs are unlikely to do any good. They are designed to attack bacteria, and, as you have seen, colds and flu are caused by viruses. The only time they may be helpful is for people, such as the elderly and those with long-term illnesses, who are at risk of getting a bacterial infection on top of their colds or flu.

There's no cure for flu. You just have to wait until your immune cells get the better of the virus.

SMOKING

The list of chest diseases caused by smoking is long and unpleasant: lung cancer, emphysema, bronchitis, mouth cancer, cancer of the larynx. Many die slow, painful deaths. They aren't all old. They are men and women of all ages.

People who smoke run high risks. Even if smoking does not kill them, it damages their lungs. They get more chest infections, they cough, wheeze, and choke. They aren't able to run as far or as fast as they should because there isn't enough oxygen going to their cells. Their breath smells and their teeth decay. And when they blow smoke over their friends, they can make them ill, too. In fact, some nonsmokers die because they have breathed in the cigarette fumes of their friends over many years.

He's not just wrecking his lungs; he's damaging her health, too.

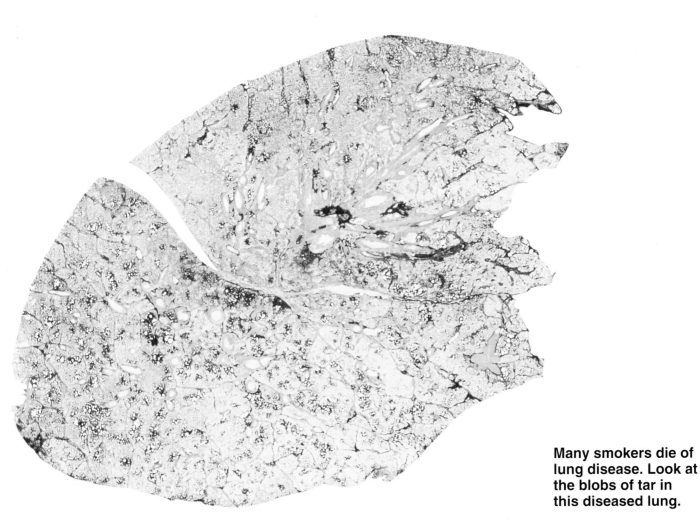

Many smokers die of lung disease. Look at the blobs of tar in this diseased lung.

Tobacco contains hundreds of chemicals. Some cause cancer. Others destroy the fragile walls of the bronchioles and the alveoli. One—carbon monoxide—pushes oxygen off the hemoglobin in the blood so that cells all over the body are starved of oxygen.

The nicotine in cigarettes is very addictive. Smokers get a physical and mental need for nicotine that only another cigarette can satisfy. If you saw inside a smoker's lungs, you'd probably be sick. You'd find dead and dying cells, globules of blackened mucus waiting to be coughed up, shriveled alveoli, scarred bronchioles, and blocked and broken blood vessels.

Yet each year thousands of young people start smoking. Once they are hooked, they find it very hard to give up. Many people want to give up smoking and some manage. But they rarely lose the craving for a cigarette.

There is no "safe" cigarette. High tar, medium tar, low tar—they can all kill people and give them lung diseases. Do you know anyone dying of lung disease? It's very frightening. So please don't be tempted to start smoking.

DEATH SMOKE

In the United States some 434,000 people die each year from the effects of cigarette smoking. That's one death every 1.2 minutes. On average, a cigarette takes five and a half minutes off your life. Smoking causes four times as many premature deaths as all other avoidable risks put together, including road accidents, alcohol abuse, drugs, and suicide.

If you stop smoking, your risk of dying returns to that of a nonsmoker within ten to fifteen years.

THE TOBACCO INDUSTRY

The tobacco industry spends millions of dollars a year advertising cigarettes, cigars and pipe tobacco, despite the fact that these can kill and injure people. If advertisements told drug addicts to share needles that would spread AIDS, there would be uproar. Yet smoking kills far more people each year than AIDS. Similarly, if supermarkets sold cyanide, we'd be horrified. Yet these stores sell cigarettes and they contain cyanide, too.

Why do some governments let tobacco companies advertise? The answer is because they get a lot of money in taxes on cigarettes. The tobacco industry also employs a lot of people. Many would lose their jobs if cigarette sales fell dramatically as a result of a ban on advertising.

In spite of this, some countries, such as France, Italy, and Portugal, have decided that smoking is so bad for your health that they have agreed to ban tobacco advertising. Governments that are against a ban argue that people will still smoke even if advertising is banned. People start smoking for many different reasons, including pressure from friends or relatives to have a cigarette. Clearly, advertising is not the only reason.

But advertising must help sales or companies wouldn't spend all that money! Advertisements show smokers as strong, tough, successful people —they also appear to be very healthy. They suggest that if you smoke, you will be successful, attractive, even desirable, too.

Although this cigarette advertisement aims to persuade you otherwise, there's not much pleasure in bad breath, gum disease, and throat cancer.

Cigarette advertising on a racing car. Whose life is at stake?

DEVELOPING COUNTRIES

In many countries advertising campaigns that promote smoking have been very successful. Recently the number of people who smoke in developing countries, such as India, China, Africa, and South America, has shot up. About 70 percent of Chinese men over twenty smoke and between the years 2020 and 2025, an estimated 2 million Chinese will die per year from smoking-related diseases such as lung cancer.

When they die, we will be partly to blame. People in developing countries often follow the example of those in the West. Smoking is seen as a sign of wealth. So people who want to show their friends that they have money buy cigarettes. Only by banning all tobacco advertising and reducing our smoking can we show people in poorer countries that it is a dangerous habit.

Who's to blame if this man dies of lung cancer? Is there anything we can do to help?

AIR POLLUTION

Even before automobiles, air pollution darkened Sheffield, England.

Londoners called it a "pea souper"—smog so thick you could barely see the person in front of you. It hung like a dirty cloud over the city. The smogs that covered big cities in the first half of this century came from levels of air pollution that would be unacceptable to us today. They were caused by the huge amounts of smoke from coal fires and factory chimneys.

Some cities still have smogs. But today they are caused by vehicle exhausts rather than coal fires. Los Angeles, Athens, Cairo, Bombay, and Mexico City are just some of the cities whose skyscrapers are often covered by smog.

Air pollution is not just ugly, it is dangerous to our health. In 1952 smog hung over London for

weeks and caused 4,000 deaths. The chemicals in smog attack the lungs. People who already have lung disorders such as bronchitis and asthma are at greatest risk. Even people with good lungs can feel breathless and uncomfortable when pollution levels are high.

Sulphur dioxide (SO_2) was the gas responsible for the London smogs of the 1950s. It is produced by power stations and diesel engines. In the lungs, it makes the bronchioles narrower so that less air can get in.

Sometimes smoke from coal fires mixes with sulphur dioxide. Smoke particles can get trapped in the lungs and cause damage, especially if they contain cancer-causing chemicals.

Nitrogen dioxide (NO_2) is one of a family of chemicals called NOX (oxides of nitrogen). They are produced when fuel is burned in cars and power stations. When these chemicals are breathed in, they irritate the lining of the bronchioles and can make breathing more difficult.

In summer, sunlight can react with NOX and hydrocarbons (also found in car exhaust) to produce ozone. Ozone irritates the lungs and makes breathing more difficult for people with asthma and other lung diseases, or those who are exercising when ozone levels are high.

Carbon monoxide is another gas found in vehicle exhaust. In large amounts it prevents the blood from carrying oxygen around the body.

When nitrogen and sulphur dioxides in the air combine with water droplets, they may form acid air, which also irritates the lungs. If they then fall to the ground as acid rain, they can badly damage plants and trees.

ABOVE It's hard to imagine life without cars. But we aren't helping the environment.

GAS MASKS

When you are exercising, you breathe faster and harder to provide your muscles with enough oxygen. However, in busy towns and cities you also breathe in large amounts of pollution from the air.

You have probably seen some cyclists, motorbike riders, and joggers wearing gas masks to protect their lungs from polluted air (right). Some of these are very effective in filtering out most of the chemicals such as NOX and SO_2 that upset the lungs.

AIR-CONDITIONING

Living and working in modern air-conditioned buildings can make us ill. More and more people wheeze and sneeze, have headaches, sore eyes, itchy skin, and feel generally unwell because of the lack of fresh air in some buildings. It's called "sick building syndrome."

There are several reasons why this happens. Microbes can live in air-conditioning ducts and may go around and around a building. So bacterial and viral infections are passed to everyone in an office. Central heating means that buildings are kept much warmer and drier than they used to be and many bugs like this.

It isn't just offices that can be "sick." Our homes may also harbor creatures that make us ill. Thick carpets instead of wooden floors attract dust mites.

A modern air-conditioned office provides a good home for many germs.

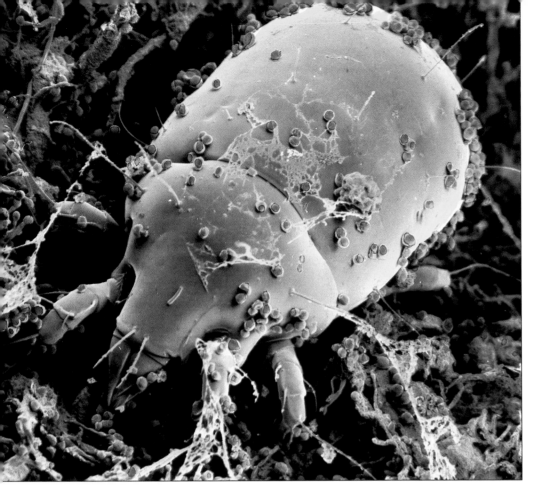

The house dust mite isn't really green. Color has been added to make it stand out. There are millions of mites in your bed, your chairs, your carpets, and your curtains—but you won't be able to see them without a microscope!

BELOW Animal fur is one of the most common causes of asthma.

These tiny little mites are related to spiders, and they are found anywhere that is warm and cozy. That means carpets, chair covers, curtains, and bedding. There is a protein in their feces that makes some people wheeze and have runny noses. In fact, more people are thought to be allergic to house dust mites than anything else.

Experts advise us to open windows and reduce the humidity of our homes—even in winter. Carpets need to be cleaned regularly and bedding washed at high temperatures to kill dust mites. If that doesn't work, it may be best to pull up carpets and put down hard floors with rugs that can easily be taken up and shaken.

OTHER ALLERGIES

Pollen and animal fur are the other two things most likely to upset the noses and lungs of people who are allergic to them. Trying to avoid them is easier said than done! But it is the best way of reducing the risk of hay fever or asthma.

If you know you are allergic to animal fur, you shouldn't really get a pet. If you already have one, at least keep it out of your bedroom and off the furniture. Don't touch your face when you are playing with your pet and always wash your hands after you've been playing with it.

CHEST DISORDERS

Sometimes a cold or a bout of flu goes down to your chest. This means that the infection has spread down into the smaller airways in your lungs and made them inflamed and sore. This is called acute bronchitis.

Some people—mostly smokers—have inflamed airways for many months at a time, especially through the winter. This is called chronic bronchitis. It may have started with a cold or flu, or the chemicals in their cigarette smoke may have made their airways inflamed and full of mucus. Sufferers feel very run-down.

Pneumonia is an infection in the alveoli. They become clogged with fluid and cells and unable to absorb oxygen normally. Young and fit people usually get over pneumonia with antibiotics.

But it can kill frail elderly people, especially those who are bedridden after a serious stroke or cancer.

Pneumonia is usually caused by a bacterium. That's why antibiotics are so effective. But sometimes it is caused by a virus and is harder to treat.

Emphysema is also a disease of the alveoli. Once again, most cases are caused by smoking, but some people have an inherited disorder that makes them prone to the disease. The alveoli become permanently damaged and unable to provide the body with enough oxygen. Drugs can help, but many people with emphysema need extra oxygen.

There is no doubt that people who smoke are more likely to have chronic bronchitis and emphysema—often both. These are very unpleasant diseases. Sufferers cough and are nearly always breathless. In the later stages of the diseases, they are too breathless even to stand up.

LEGIONNAIRES' DISEASE

In 1976, a group of former soldiers (members of the American Legion) were struck down by severe pneumonia. The type of bacterium that caused the outbreak was called Legionella, and all outbreaks that have happened since have been called Legionnaires' disease. Like other forms of pneumonia, it responds to antibiotics but is more serious in old people.

Legionnaires' disease is not spread from person to person but is caught by breathing infected water droplets from air-conditioning systems. Each outbreak attracts a lot of publicity because people get frightened that the bacterium may be in their ventilation systems, too.

These are the bacteria that cause Legionnaires' disease — a kind of pneumonia.

RIGHT The X ray of a chest showing pneumonia in the right lung

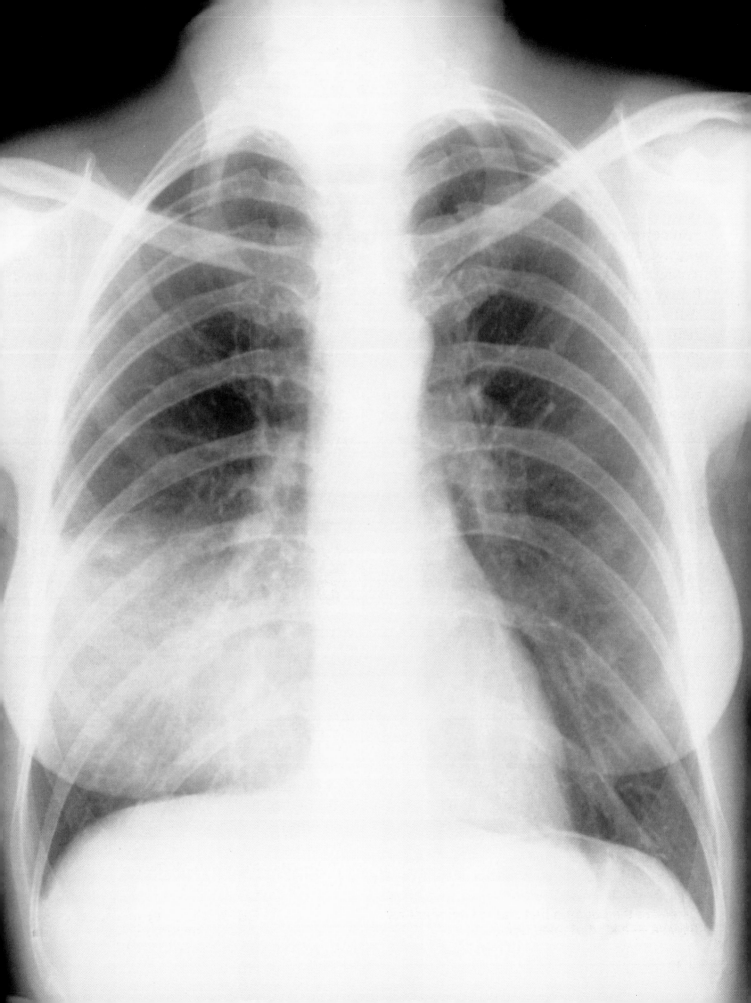

ASTHMA

One in ten children has asthma. The muscles in the walls of their airways contract when they shouldn't. Their tubes get narrower so less air can get in and out of the lungs. Their alveoli are working as hard as they can. But there simply isn't enough air for them to process.

As carbon dioxide begins to build up in the blood, the brain sends signals to the lungs to breathe faster. They try, but they still can't satisfy the body's needs. Breathing becomes very inefficient—lots of quick, shallow, noisy breaths. This noise is called wheezing.

There are several reasons why the muscles in the airways contract and cause an asthma attack. Many asthmatics are allergic to things in the air. Their immune systems, which normally protect them from infection, overreact to harmless things like pollen, dust, and animal fur. These immune cells set off a chain of events, which results in the airways getting narrower.

Some asthmatics even overreact to things like cold air or cigarette smoke. Their airways immediately seize up and they start to wheeze.

Luckily, asthma doesn't have to stop you from doing the things you want to. Cricketer Ian Botham and Olympic swimmer Adrian Moorhouse are just two of many sports people who have reached the top despite their asthma. There are plenty of successful businesspeople, actors, doctors, and dancers who also have asthma. This is because there are plenty of very effective drugs that can be taken to open up airways and stop wheezing or prevent the immune system from overreacting to things in the first place.

Olympic swimmer Adrian Moorhouse shows that asthma hasn't stopped him!

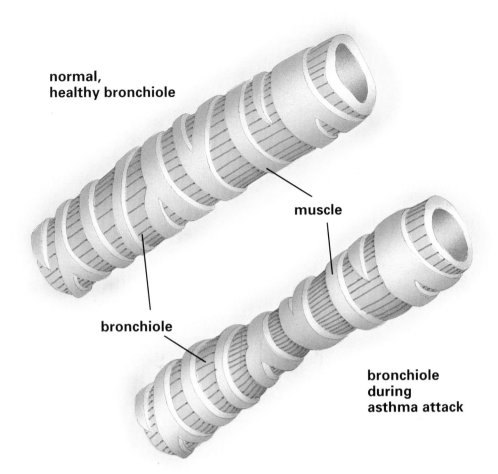

normal,
healthy bronchiole

muscle

bronchiole

bronchiole
during
asthma attack

LEFT In asthma, muscle wrapped around the bronchioles contracts, narrowing the airway and restricting air flow so it becomes hard to breathe.

BELOW A quick puff with her inhaler and this girl will soon be able to play with her friends again.

INHALED STEROIDS

Most asthma experts now believe that it is important not just to relieve asthma symptoms when they happen but to get at the cause. When the immune cells see something they don't like, they don't just make the airways close up. The airways also become inflamed and too much mucus is produced. This can go on for a long time and eventually it will leave scars on the walls of the airways.

It is now possible to take drugs that reduce this inflammation. They are called steroids. You can inhale them straight into the lungs—just like other drugs that make the airways wider.

Some people worry about taking steroids. But when they are inhaled, they are very unlikely to cause any problems. And they are very effective at preventing the airways from becoming inflamed.

TUBERCULOSIS

Before drugs were discovered that could kill TB bacteria, people believed in "touching" by kings as a form of treatment. Charles II (pictured here in a drawing from 1654) had a particularly good reputation.

Tuberculosis (TB) was the scourge of the eighteenth and nineteenth centuries and the first half of the twentieth century. Every year, millions of people worldwide died of the dreaded disease. No family was left untouched. In 1882, the German scientist Robert Koch discovered microbes in the lungs of people with TB. But it wasn't until the early 1950s that drugs were discovered that could kill the bacteria and save many lives.

Before that, fresh air and rest were the main treatments. Men and women with TB were sent to hospitals in mountain regions, where the air was believed to be cleaner.

The bacterium that causes TB can attack any organ of the body, but the lungs are its usual target.

The microbe gets into the lungs and is soon surrounded by immune cells trying to destroy it. This mixture of bacterial and human cells is called a tubercle. Tubercles join together and some of the lung tissue caught in the middle dies. Sometimes the lung heals, but without treatment large areas may be destroyed. This can be fatal.

Modern drugs can stop the TB microbe in its tracks. In the 1950s and 1960s, doctors in mobile vans X-rayed thousands of people to find those infected with TB so that they could receive the new treatment. And schoolchildren were given injections against the bacterium. In fact, TB is widespread in many developing countries and recurring in many developed countries.

PREVENTING INFECTION

TB is especially found in many Western countries among people in Asian and African communities. They were infected with the bacterium before they left their own countries and can pass it on to their families and friends. It is important that these people are found quickly before too much lung damage is done. The infection cannot always be treated easily and effectively with drugs. Those people who are not infected can be immunized against the microorganism that causes TB.

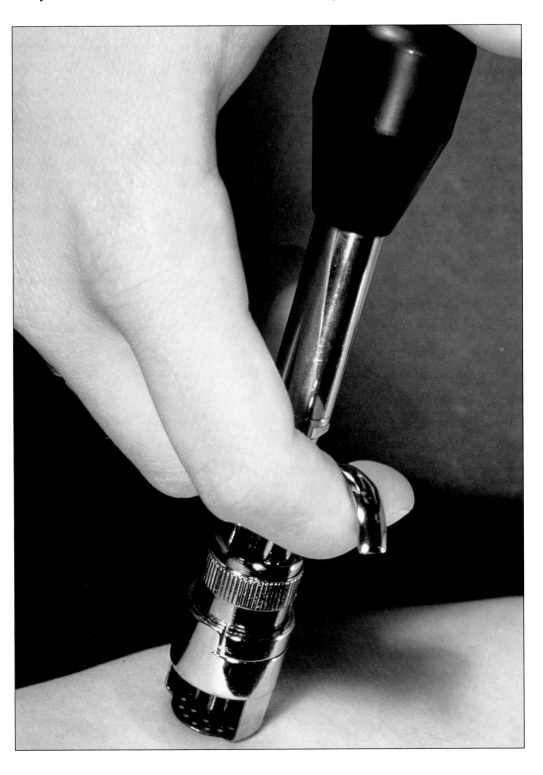

Today, children are routinely immunized against TB. First, they are tested to see if they have any immunity to the bacterium (as in the picture). If they don't, they are given the vaccine.

CYSTIC FIBROSIS

Cystic fibrosis is the most common serious inherited disease. Children with cystic fibrosis produce too much mucus in their lungs, and most lack important enzymes that they need to be able to digest their food. The extra mucus makes them prone to serious chest infections.

Each of our cells contains all the genetic material —DNA—that controls what we look like and what sort of person we are. But some of these genes may be faulty. We inherit two copies of most of our genes—one from each parent. Children who inherit a cystic fibrosis gene from one of their parents will not get the disease. But they may pass it on to their children. One in twenty-five people is a carrier of the abnormal gene that causes cystic fibrosis. Only children who inherit the bad gene from both their parents get the disease.

Good drugs and regular physiotherapy to get rid of some of the mucus have meant that people with cystic fibrosis do much better now than even ten years ago. They can also take digestive enzymes to replace those that are missing. And, at the first sign of a chest infection, they are given antibiotics.

Some children with cystic fibrosis have had heart and lung transplants to replace their diseased lungs. It is easier to transplant the lungs and heart together than the lungs alone. So the healthy heart of the cystic fibrosis patient can be given to someone else who needs just a heart.

Children who have had transplants do very well. They still need their extra digestive enzymes, but their new lungs are normal. All of those who have had the operation are being carefully checked to see how well they do as they grow up.

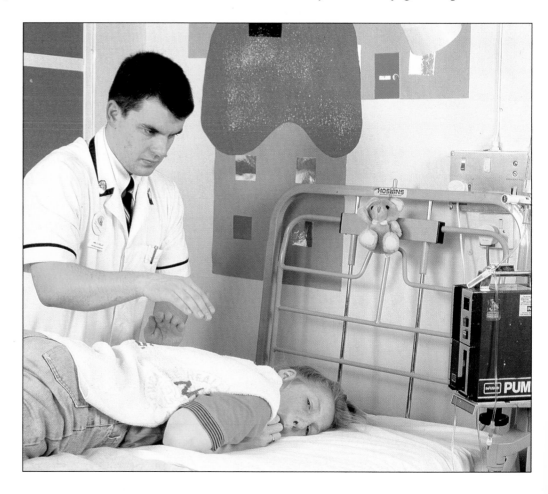

Daily physiotherapy for a girl with cystic fibrosis helps to dislodge the mucus in her lungs so she can cough it up. There is then less chance of her lungs becoming infected.

A gene therapist at work in his laboratory

FINDING THE GENE

The gene that causes cystic fibrosis was discovered in 1989. This wouldn't have been possible without the scientific advances of the last ten years. In the end, researchers hope to find out the job of all 50,000 genes in each of our cells.

If doctors know what they should do, they may be able to treat the genes so that they all work properly. This is called gene therapy. A few people have already had gene therapy for very severe diseases of the immune system. Before long, doctors could be using gene therapy to treat diseases such as cystic fibrosis. In the meantime, they will continue to use a combination of drugs, physiotherapy, enzymes, and transplants.

ANESTHETIC GASES

Before the days of anesthetics, operations could be extremely painful.

It's hard to imagine having an operation without an anesthetic to deaden the pain. But until the middle of the nineteenth century that's exactly what happened. Operations were carried out as quickly as possible so that patients weren't in pain for too long.

In 1844, nitrous oxide (N_2O) was the first gas to be used successfully as an anesthetic during the removal of a tooth. It is still widely used today with oxygen, to keep people asleep during surgical operations.

Gases like nitrous oxide and, later, ether, chloroform, and halothane, could only be used after doctors understood how the lungs worked. During the eighteenth century they began to understand what happens to the air that we breathe in.

Before it was used as an anesthetic, nitrous oxide was used as a social drug, much like alcohol today. It was called laughing gas because when people breathed it in, they felt much happier and started to laugh.

In 1846, ether was the first gas to be used in a major operation—to remove a tumor. But ether catches fire easily, and people who breathe it in are very sick when they wake up from their operation. So doctors looked for other drugs that had fewer unpleasant side effects.

Today, halothane and nitrous oxide are probably the most widely used anesthetic gases. They don't, of course, put you to sleep by working on the lungs. They get into the blood, via the alveoli, and are transported around the body to parts of the brain that control consciousness.

Usually, anesthetic gases are used with other anesthetic drugs that are injected directly into the bloodstream. This is because doctors have found that if they use several different drugs they can use less of each one. So people wake up more quickly after their operations and are able to be up and around sooner.

In fact, many operations are now done under local anesthetic. This means that the patient stays awake but feels no pain.

ANESTHETICS IN CHILDBIRTH

We have England's Queen Victoria to thank for making the use of anesthetics in childbirth acceptable. She used chloroform to get herself through the birth of her son Prince Leopold in 1853. Ever since, women have been able to have drugs to relieve the pain of having a baby.

Some choose a mixture of nitrous oxide and oxygen, while others have drugs that are injected into their bloodstream.

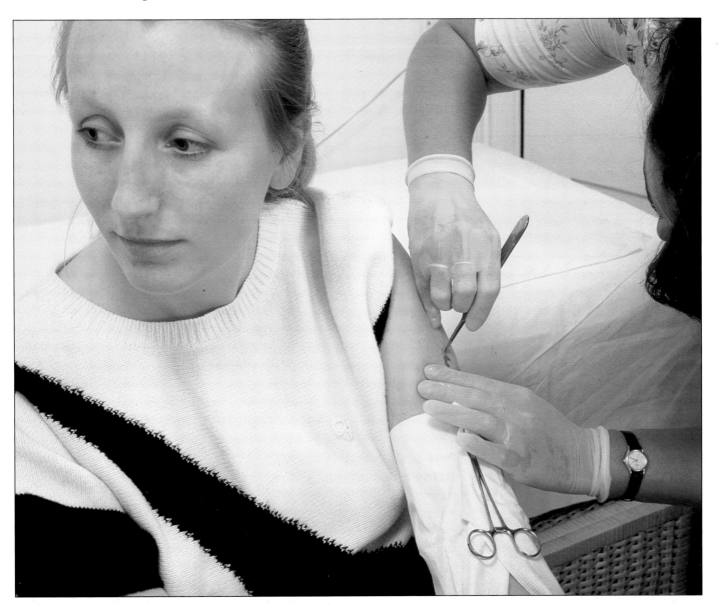

This woman is having a wart removed under local anesthetic. She can't feel a thing.

ARTIFICIAL RESPIRATION

Each year, thousands of people owe their lives to a machine that acts as a pair of lungs for them. Premature babies, car accident victims, and people who have had major operations are just some of those who need a respirator. The alveoli in their lungs are able to absorb oxygen from the air and get rid of carbon dioxide. But for some reason the muscles in their chests are unable to make the lungs inflate and deflate, so they can't inhale and exhale properly.

The muscles of tiny premature babies are simply too weak for them to breathe on their own. People who have been in car accidents or have had major operations may be so deeply unconscious that their brains stop sending messages to the muscles in their chests telling them to breathe.

The respirator is a machine that breathes for you. A tube that is attached to the respirator goes down through the mouth or nose and into the lungs. Air is then pumped down the tube to inflate the lungs and provide much-needed oxygen.

The rate at which the lungs are inflated and deflated and the amounts of oxygen and carbon dioxide in the bloodstream are continuously monitored to be sure that the patient is getting the right amount of air.

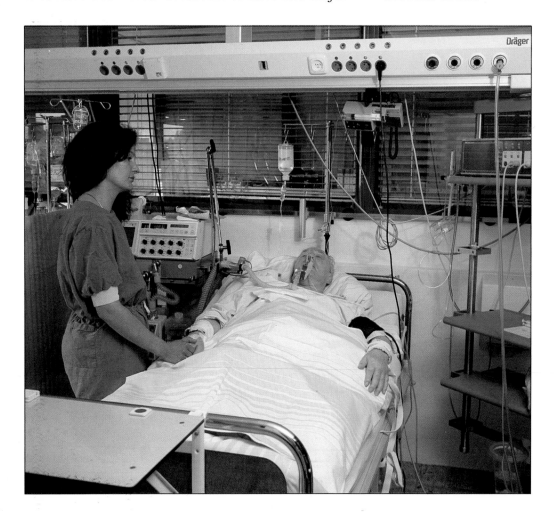

LEFT A respirator keeps this man's lungs working while he recovers from a heart attack.

OPPOSITE The man at the back of the picture is lying in an iron lung to help him breathe. The woman in the wheelchair has a more advanced device that allows her to move around while her lungs are artificially inflated and deflated.

People who need artificial respiration are usually treated in the intensive care unit of a hospital. Some people remain unconscious—in a coma—for months. Respirators can go on breathing for them all that time. Others gradually come out of their comas and start to breathe again for themselves.

Sometimes it becomes clear that a person will never come out of his or her coma because the brain is too badly damaged. His or her relatives may then decide to switch off the respirator so that he or she can die peacefully. Obviously this is a heartrending decision to have to make.

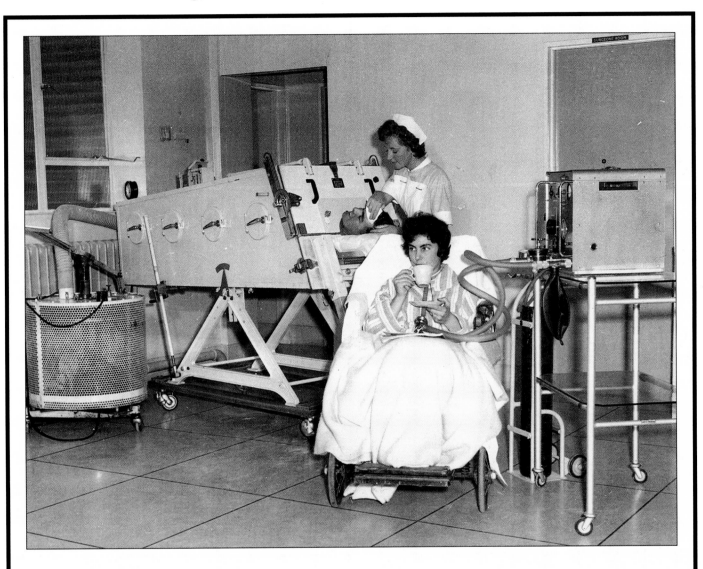

IRON LUNGS

Today's respirators were developed from the original "iron lungs" that were used to keep polio victims alive during the epidemic that occurred in the 1950s.

People with polio became paralyzed and could not move. In the worst cases, their chest muscles stopped working. The iron lung was developed to make them breathe. Instead of air being pumped down into their lungs, their bodies were placed in large tanks with only their heads poking out. When air inside the tank was sucked out, their lungs inflated and air was taken in through their mouths. Air was then pumped back into the tanks so that the increased pressure on the outside of their chests pushed their lungs flat and air was breathed out.

Fortunately, most of the people who survived polio were left only partly paralyzed, and in the end they were able to breathe again without their iron lungs.

BETTER BREATHING

How long can you hold your breath? Most people can do it for between thirty and fifty seconds. If you take several quick, deep breaths first, you will be able to hold your breath for longer. This is because the amount of carbon dioxide in your blood will go down. So it will be longer before your brain orders your lungs to inflate.

You can do this as a short experiment on dry land. But you should be careful about holding your breath underwater. Some people have drowned because their brain allowed them to hold their breath for too long. They had too little oxygen in their blood and lost consciousness before they could get to the surface.

Some mammals, such as seals, can stay underwater without taking a breath for up to fifteen minutes. But their red blood cells can carry more oxygen, and, as they dive, their heart rate goes down and blood only goes to vital organs. So they need less oxygen.

If you climb above about 10,000 feet, you will notice that you get out of breath more easily. You may even feel sick and dizzy. This is because there is less oxygen in the air at this level than there is nearer sea level.

As the body tries to make up for the shortfall, you breathe more quickly. This has precisely the wrong effect. By breathing faster, the amount of carbon dioxide in your blood falls and your brain thinks you do not need to breathe. You soon feel very ill.

People who go higher and higher without waiting for their bodies to get used to the altitude become very sick and may even die. What they should do is spend a few days at the higher altitude and wait for their bodies to get used to the air. After a few days the bone marrow will start producing more red blood cells so more oxygen can be carried around the body.

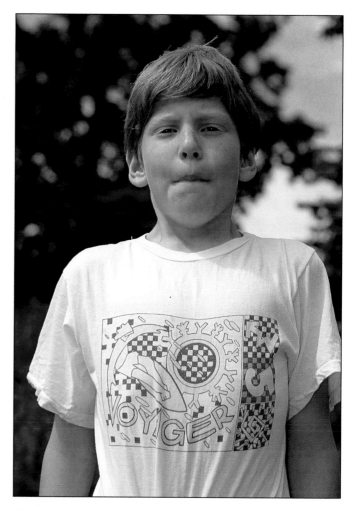

How long do you think this boy will be able to hold his breath? About thirty seconds? Be careful when holding your breath—it can be quite dangerous!

Athletes who want to perform better train at a high altitude so that they can carry more oxygen in their blood. If their competition is at sea level—with normal amounts of oxygen in the air—they will then be at an advantage because they can get extra oxygen to their muscles. This means they can move faster and keep going for longer.

Altitude training can help improve an athlete's performance on the big day.

WHAT TO DO IF SOMEONE STOPS BREATHING

If you are with a third person send them to get help.

● To help someone breathe, turn him or her onto the back. Tip the head back, open the mouth, and check that there is nothing blocking the throat. Pinch the nose shut. Take a deep breath and place your mouth over his or hers. Blow strongly into the lungs.

● Take another deep breath and breathe out into his or her lungs. Keep doing this every five seconds. Between each breath, listen for air coming out of the person's mouth and watch the chest fall. Go on breathing into the mouth until he or she starts to breathe again or help arrives.

DOES ALL LIFE NEED OXYGEN?

It's impossible for us to imagine life without oxygen. If the oxygen supply to the brain stops for more than a few moments, cells start to die. Within two to three minutes the damage is irreversible.

You probably know that on earth, plants replace all the oxygen used up by animals. They convert carbon dioxide and water into carbohydrates and oxygen. The process is called photosynthesis. We don't know of any other planets that have enough oxygen for life as we know it. It is possible that there are other forms of life that don't need oxygen to live. But life on earth has evolved over millions of years to use oxygen in its cells, and we can't change that. Even small changes in the gases that we breathe can make us ill.

It is unlikely that we will ever "run out" of oxygen. But levels of carbon dioxide and some pollutant gases in the air are rising. If this goes on, more people will suffer from lung diseases.

If we treat our lungs badly, we will suffer. And what we do to our air today will affect generations of people who live after us.

RIGHT The devastation caused by acid rain

OPPOSITE Lush forest in the Malaysian jungle helps produce oxygen to sustain life on this planet.

GLOSSARY

allergy reaction of the immune system to a harmless substance that may cause wheezing and runny noses.

alveoli tiny air sacs in the lung where oxygen is absorbed into the blood and carbon dioxide removed.

antibiotic a drug that kills bacteria.

bacterium a germ.

bronchiole small airway in the lung, which leads into an alveolus.

bronchitis swelling of the bronchi or bronchioles caused by an infection or by irritant chemicals.

bronchus one of two large airways that lead from the trachea into the lungs.

capillary tiny blood vessel from which gases pass into and out of cells.

cystic fibrosis serious inherited lung disease.

diaphragm the sheet of muscle below the lungs that is important for breathing.

emphysema serious lung disease of the alveoli.

hemoglobin red coloring in red blood cells, which carry oxygen around the body.

intercostal muscle between the ribs.

larynx voice box.

NOX (oxides of nitrogen) pollutant chemicals in the air.

pharynx throat.

pneumonia serious infection of the lungs caused by a bacterium or a virus.

surfactant the slippery fluid in the airways that makes breathing easier.

trachea tube that carries air from the throat to the bronchi.

tuberculosis (TB) serious bacterial infection, usually of the lungs, which still occurs in some developed countries.

virus tiny germ that causes colds and flu and many other infections.

BOOKS TO READ

Childbirth. Fern G. Brown, New York: Franklin Watts, 1988.

Communicable Diseases. Thomas H. Metos. New York: Franklin Watts, 1987.

Everything You Need to Know about Smoking. Elizabeth Keyishian. New York: The Rosen Group, 1989.

Focus on Nicotine and Caffeine. Robert Perry. New York: Twenty-First Century Books, 1990.

The Lungs and Breathing. Revised Edition. Steve Parker. New York: Franklin Watts, 1989.

A Reference Guide to Clean Air. Cass R. Sandak. Hillside, NJ: Enslow Publishers, 1990.

Smoking. Lila Gano. San Diego: Lucent Books, 1989.

Smoking. Sherry Sonnett. Revised Edition. Edited by Lorna Greenberg. New York: Franklin Watts, 1989.

The Respiratory System. Mary Kittredge. New York: Chelsea House, 1989.

ACKNOWLEDGMENTS

All Sport 12 (Gary Mortimore), 32 (Tony Duffy), 43 (top, Ancil Nance); Chapel Studios 10, 21; Eye Ubiquitous 11 (top, Helene Rogers), 14 (Mostyn 92), 18 (bottom, Helene Rogers), 21 (Helene Rogers), 24 (T. Baverstock), 25 (bottom, Julia Waterlow), 42 (Yiorgus Nikiteas); Explorer 14; Life Science Images cover background; Mary Evans Picture Library 26; Planet Earth cover and title page; Reflections 13 (bottom, J. Woodcock); Science Photo Library 4 (CNRI), 5 (Peter Menzel), 7 (top, Biophoto Associates/bottom, Simon Fraser/Princess Mary Hospital, Newcastle), 8 (Dr. Tony Brain), 9 (CNRI), 19 (Dr. Gary Settles), 20 (top, CNRI/bottom NIBSC), 22 (Sheila Terry), 23 (James Stevenson), 27 (bottom, Jo Pasieka), 29 (top, CNRI), 30 (Barry Dowsett), 31, 33 (John Durham), 34 (Dr. J. Burgess), 35 (Biophoto Associates), 36 (Simon Fraser/RVI, Newcastle-upon-Tyne), 37 (Will and Demi McIntyre), 38, 39 (Hattie Young), 43 (bottom, Blair Seitz); Skjold 10, 11 (bottom); The Environmental Picture Library 44 (Paul Glendell), 45 (C. Jones); Topham 13 (top), 17, 28, 41; WPL 10, 29 (bottom, Julia Davey); Zefa 6 (J. Feingersh), 11 (bottom, N. Schaefer), 13 (top and bottom), 15 (Pelegic Eye), 16, 18 (top), 25 (top), 27 (top, Dr. Mueller), 40.
Artwork: Malcolm S. Walker.

INDEX